Acknowledgment:

"I am grateful for all the support and encouragement provided by Mom, Dad, Nan, Pop, Grae, and Daniel".

Author Bio:

Hope Hickman is a newly published author from Albany, New York. Hope's academic background is broad, loving sciences and math, but has always had a passion for the arts. Currently, she graduated from SUNY Brockport, Newyork with a B.S. degree in Business Administration.

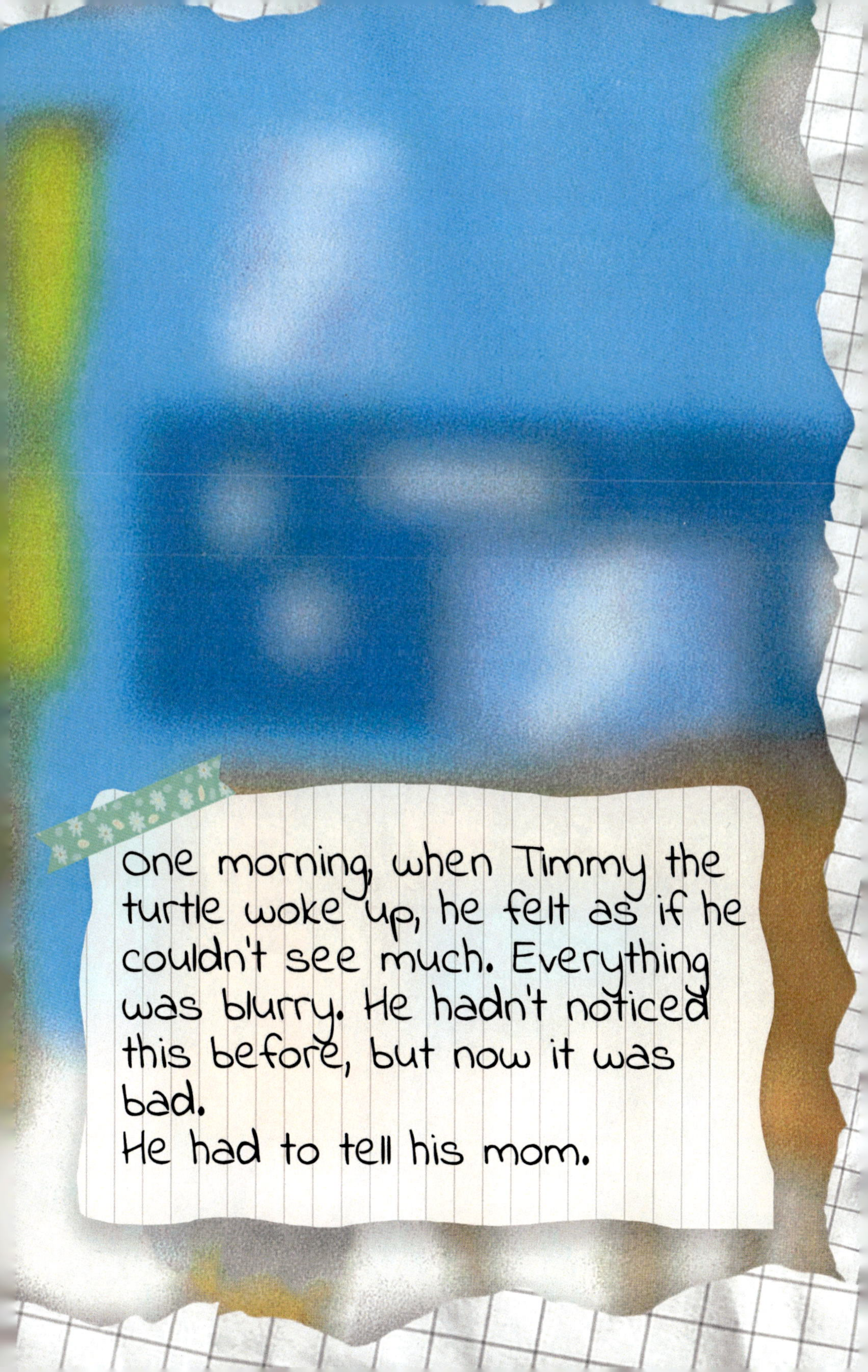

One morning, when Timmy the turtle woke up, he felt as if he couldn't see much. Everything was blurry. He hadn't noticed this before, but now it was bad.
He had to tell his mom.

Timmy ran to his mom exclaiming,
"Mom! Mom!, i can't see..everything is blurry"

His mom replied to him saying,
"oh no! maybe we should get you some glasses!"

Timmy's mom brought him to the doctor where Timmy tried on all different shapes and sizes of glasses! He tried **square ones**, but didn't like them. He tried **rectangular ones**, but didn't like those either. He tried **triangular ones**, but didn't like those either! Then, he tried on the **circle glasses.** He loved them but worried what everyone at school would think!

Timmy went to school the next day, nervous about what everyone would say.

He ran into one of his old friends, Bailey, the bird, and her friends. Bailey and all her friends wore square glasses.

Before he could even ask if they liked his new glasses, they all started to make fun of him, telling him,

"Those glasses look weird,"

and calling him names. **"Hey, four eyes!"** they all said, laughing. This made Timmy really sad.

Timmy walked away from them because they made him sad. He then saw his other friend, Flynn the fish, wearing triangular glasses. He ran to Flynn to show him his new glasses.

He thought Flynn would like them, but instead, Flynn laughed and said things to him like,

"Hey, googly eyes!"

Timmy became even more sad and ran into the bathroom.

Timmy thought everyone would love his glasses as much as he did. He heard the bathroom door open and peeked through his stall to see his friend Suzy the skunk, sitting there.

"Are you in there, Timmy?" said Suzy.
"Yes," replied Timmy.
"I love your glasses," exclaimed Suzy.
"Anyone that disagrees is just jealous!"
"You think so?" questioned Timmy"I do.
They look so cool," Suzy said convincingly.
"When I first got my glasses, people made fun of me too. But now everyone likes them."

in this lifetime
how on earth does
little things matter
rashing down aro
far away from the
trouble with crop
were make
f black an
were
unlike the first and se
tably
being to be an

Timmy went home later that day and told his mom what had happened. He explained how Bailey and Flynn had been rude when he thought they were friends. Timmy questioned whether he bought the right glasses and explained to his mom how he no longer wanted to wear them because nobody liked them. His mom shook her head in sadness.

"They must just be jealous because those glasses look SOOO good. Besides, it doesn't matter what they think. As long as you like them, that's all that matters!"

exclaimed Timmy's mom.

"That's what Suzy said, too. Maybe you guys are right,"

Timmy pointed out.

Timmy went up to bed after he and his mom talked. That night, Timmy fell asleep, happy about his glasses no matter what th people at school said.

The next morning, when Timmy woke up, he got dressed, put his glasses on and left for school. when he arrived there, he noticed that EVERYONE was wearing round glasses just like his, even Flynn and Bailey.

He walked up to Bailey and Flynn, who happened to be standing together, and asked why they were wearing glasses just like his.

"We're sorry for making fun of you," Bailey and Flynn explained together. **"We were just jealous because the round glasses are so cool, but we only have the square and triangle ones."**

Timmy smiled,
"It's okay, guys. It upset me that you didn't like them, but I'm glad you like them now. You both look SUPER good in them!"

Timmy then saw Suzy and ran up to her.

"Everyone is wearing my glasses!"

Timmy said excitedly.

"I know. I told you they all liked them, even if they didn't show it at first,"

Suzy explained.

"Thank you, Suzy!"

Timmy went home later that day and told his mom about it. He explained how everyone comes in with round glasses instead of normal square and triangle ones. He told her all the compliments he was getting and that they apologized to him for being mean. Timmy's mom was so excited to hear this. She was glad he was happy and liked his glasses.

Made in the USA
Las Vegas, NV
29 October 2024

10727542R10017